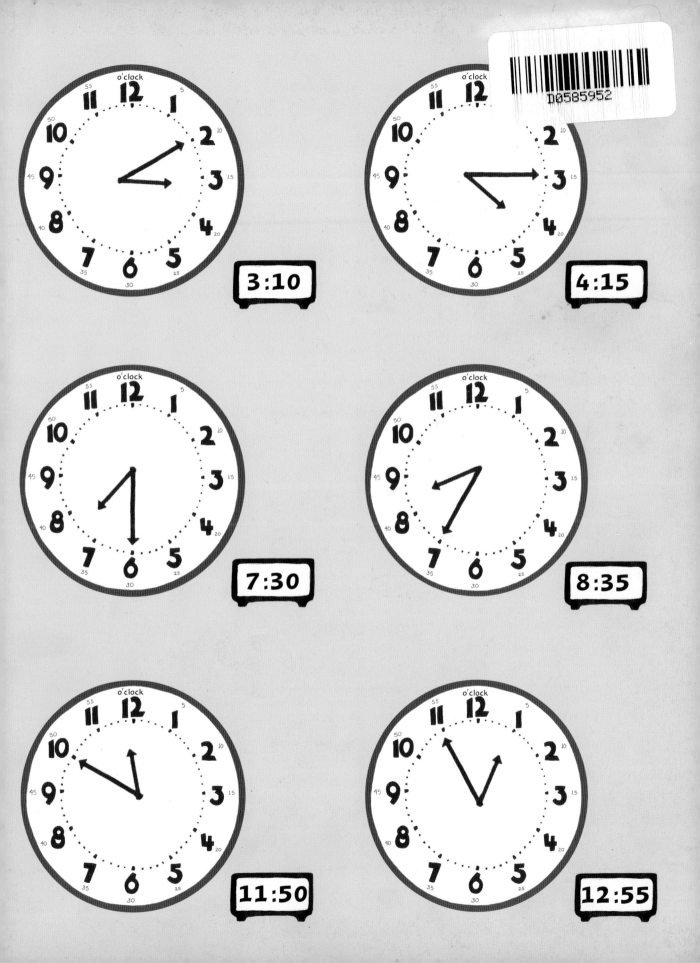

3:10

4:15

7:30

8:35

11:50

12:55

For Aidan, Lucca, Cecilia and William.
Oh, how the time flies.

Many thanks to my mother, Mary Hays,

my husband, Robert Mantho,

Victoria Wells Arms and Scottie Brower

for all of their precious time.

And a special thanks to the Vermont Arts Council.

First published in Great Britain in 2006 by Bloomsbury Publishing Plc
36 Soho Square, London, W1D 3QY

A CIP catalogue record of this book is available from the British Library

ISBN 0 7475 7645 9
ISBN-13 9780747576457

All papers used by Bloomsbury Publishing are natural, recyclable products made from wood grown in well-managed forests.
The manufacturing processes conform to the environmental regulations of the country of origin.

Printed by Leo Paper Products, China

1 3 5 7 9 10 8 6 4 2

www.bloomsbury.com/childrens

CLOCKWISE

· A Time-Telling Tale ·

SARA PINTO

BLOOMSBURY
CHILDREN'S
BOOKS

Thomas was part of a busy, busy family.

There was always something to do or somewhere to go.

Because Thomas's family was so busy, his parents were always talking about time. But Thomas couldn't tell the time. It just made him confused.

"Wake up! It's quarter past seven!"

"Do you know what time it is?"

"Hurry up and eat! It's already eight!"

Thomas decided he needed to know how to tell the time.
He stared at the kitchen clock.
"What time is it?" he asked his mum.
"Eight fifteen," she answered. Thomas didn't see a fifteen on the clock.
"What time do we have to leave?" he asked.
"Eight twenty," she answered. Thomas didn't see a twenty on the clock,
either. Telling the time is hard, thought Thomas.

The next day, while Thomas and his mother were rushing around doing errands, he saw exactly what he needed: a clock shop. "Stop the car!" shouted Thomas.

When he opened the door, Thomas heard *tick, tock, tick, tock*.
"Hello?" whispered Thomas.
"May I help you?" asked the clockmaker.
"Yes," said Thomas. "I need to learn how to tell the time."

"Then you've come to the right place," the clockmaker said.

"There are many different ways to learn,
but let me tell you about my favourite."

minute hand (long hand)
hour hand (short hand)

STANDARD CLOCK

hour hand

LEARNING CLOCK

"Clocks have two hands," she began. "The hands point to the numbers to tell us what time it is. The SHORT hand tells us the HOURS and the LONG hand tells us the MINUTES. The hands and the numbers work together to tell us the time."

The clockmaker pointed to a strange-looking clock on the wall.

"I think it's easiest to start with a clock that has just the hour hand on it. We start learning to tell the time by telling the HOURS of the day."

"When the SHORT hand points to a number, that's what HOUR it is. Of course, the hour hand doesn't always point exactly to a number. Sometimes it's before or after the number.
That means it's either BEFORE or AFTER that hour.

For instance, if the hour hand is BEFORE the three, it's BEFORE three o'clock.

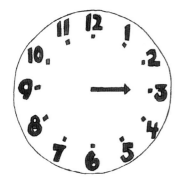

If it's pointing EXACTLY at the three, it's EXACTLY three o'clock.

If it's pointing AFTER the three, it's AFTER three o'clock.

The hand goes all the way around, always moving in the same direction, which we call CLOCKWISE."

Just then, Thomas's mum popped her head in the door.
"Thomas dear, we're late! It's half past and the girls have
finished their dance class."
"Half past?" Thomas asked.

"The way people talk about time can make it very confusing," said the clockmaker. "So, for now let's keep it simple. Learn the hours first, then you can tackle the minutes."

Confusing

4:45

six fifteen

6:36

quarter to

a.m.

ten to

four thirty

half past

8:10

p.m.

midnight

noon

Simple

After seven

Almost eleven

Around two

Six o'clock

"Here," said the clockmaker, handing Thomas a box.
"This is a one-handed clock you can practise with.
Add the minute hand once you understand the hours."
Thomas thanked the clockmaker and said goodbye.

That evening before bed, Thomas's mum helped him put up his clock. It was seven o'clock, so Thomas's mum moved the hour hand so it pointed exactly to the seven. Thomas looked at the hand. "It's not moving," said Thomas.

"Yes it is, honey," said his mum. "But it moves so slowly that you don't really notice it. It takes one whole hour for it to move from one number to the next."

Thomas lay in bed, staring at the clock. He was excited about learning to tell the time. But soon his eyelids grew heavy and he fell asleep.

The next morning when Thomas opened his eyes,
the first thing he did was look at his clock.
It looked like this:

Okay, thought Thomas, that must mean it's after seven.
Just then, his mother shouted up the stairs.
"Kids, it's time to get up! It's after seven!"
Oh good, thought Thomas, this is working.

Over the next few weeks, Thomas got better and better
at using his clock. Time was beginning to take shape.

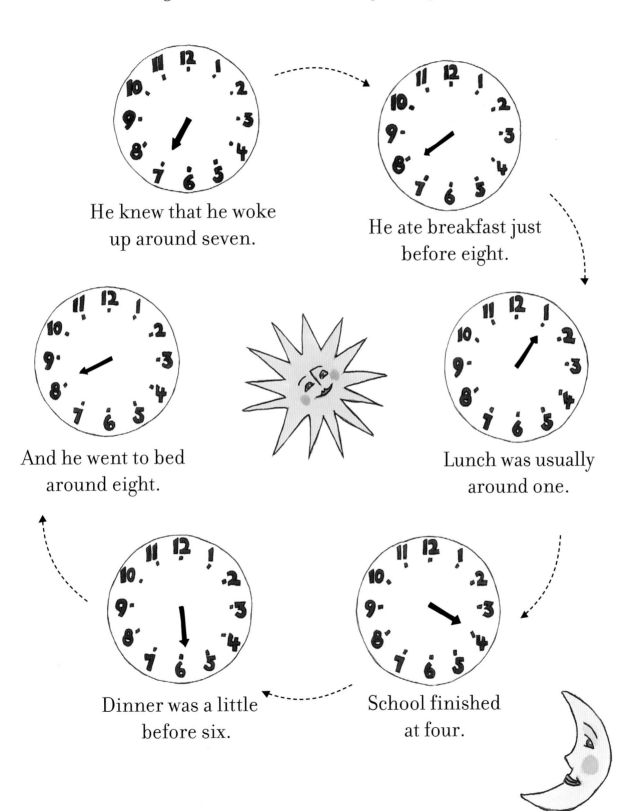

He knew that he woke
up around seven.

He ate breakfast just
before eight.

And he went to bed
around eight.

Lunch was usually
around one.

Dinner was a little
before six.

School finished
at four.

Before long, Thomas was ready for minutes!

Thomas and his mum added the minute hand to his clock.
"Can you count in fives up to sixty?" his mother asked.
"Yes," said Thomas. "Why?"
"Because there are SIXTY MINUTES in an HOUR. We use the hour
numbers to count the minutes in fives. A new hour begins when
the minute hand points to the twelve.

Let's write the minute numbers next to the hour numbers
to help you remember. When the minute hand points to
those numbers, that's how many minutes past the hour it is."

Thomas stared at the clock. "What are those little things between the numbers?" he asked his mum.

"Those marks help us keep track of the minutes, too," she answered. "Instead of writing all sixty numbers on the clock, there are sixty marks. There is a number for every five marks. So when the minute hand points to one of these marks, we just look at the big number closest to it. That helps us work out the exact minute."

They practised by moving the minute hand clockwise around the clock.

Nine fifty-four

Eleven fifteen

Twelve o'clock

Five nineteen

Eight thirty

First Thomas said the HOUR, then he said the MINUTES.
When the minute hand reached the twelve, he always said O'CLOCK.
When the minute hand reached the six, he could say it was HALF PAST
the hour, because the minute hand had gone exactly HALFWAY around
the clock. Now Thomas could keep track of minutes, too!

He worked out that if he did certain things at certain times,
he could get downstairs by seven thirty:

Up at 7.00

Wake the girls at 7.10

Hit the bathroom at 7.15

Dressed at 7.25

Downstairs by 7.30

Thomas loved the feeling
that telling the time gave him.
Master of his own destiny!
Commander of his own ship!
On time for breakfast!

Thomas's family was still a busy one, but now Thomas had time on his side. And that was a great feeling!